Wendy the Witch

Karen Dolby

Wendy the Witch

Karen Dolby

Illustrated by Brenda Haw

Editor: Michelle Bates
Series Editor: Gaby Waters

Contents

4 In the Head's Office

6 George's Good Idea

8 The Spell Library

10 Star Flight

12 Mysterious Map

14 Mountain Maze

16 Ice Cavern

18 The Key to the Castle

20 Inside the Castle

22 The Book of Special Spells

24 The Enchanted Forest

26 Lift Off!

28 Granny's Test

30 Granny Gets it Right

31 Answers

This is George and Lily and their granny, Wendy. Granny Wendy is just like anyone else's granny except that she looks a bit different. That's because she's learning to be a witch.

Granny Wendy has a problem. She hasn't been doing very well in her spellcraft classes and now she's been called in to see the Head Witch.

HEAD'S OFFICE

In the Head's Office

Granny was in trouble. The Head Wizard was there as well as the Head Witch. This was serious.

"I'm afraid your spell work has not reached the mark," the Head Witch began.

"We know you try hard, but we can only give you one last chance," said the Head Wizard. "You will have to take a spell test tomorrow at 12 o'clock."

TEST SPELLS
1 Pull a rabbit from a cauldron.
2 Get your broomstick to hover.
3 Make someone invisible.
4 Find and perform your own special spell.

BROOM STICK STAND

Percy's hat class1a

"Here are a list of the spells you must perform," the Head Wizard explained. "If you get them right you will become a proper witch at last. But if you fail, you will have to hand back your witch's hat and broomstick."

Granny hastily gathered her belongings. "Oops," she muttered. In her hurry, she had dropped a vital piece of her witchy equipment.

What had Granny Wendy dropped?

George's Good Idea

"Don't worry, Granny," said Lily, trying to cheer her up. "We'll help you with your spells."

"Start with the rabbit," George suggested, opening Granny Wendy's spellbook. "That looks easy enough."

Easy?

Not for Granny.

"As soon as she uttered the magic words there was a terrible smell and leaping frogs everywhere. But there was no sign of a rabbit.

"Perhaps you'll do better with your own special spell," said Lily hopefully.

"Mmmm," muttered Granny Wendy. "A special spell. If only I knew where to find one."

"What you need is a special spell book," said George. "Isn't there a library you can go to?"

"Of course. The Spell Library!" cried Granny Wendy. "What a brilliant idea, George. Now what did I do with my library card?" She turned out her pockets and rummaged through her bag, picked up the cat and checked under her hat. But the vital yellow card was nowhere to be found.

Can you find the library card?

The Spell Library

Granny Wendy, George and Lily set off down the high street and across the square until they came to a building that looked just like a normal library.

George couldn't help feeling disappointed as he looked at the other people going inside. They looked so ordinary. "Are they really wizards and witches?" he asked. "You'd never guess."

"Every one of them," said Granny Wendy. "They're in disguise, you see."

Inside, there were lots of books with recipes for spells, but most were very complicated and not very special. Before long, Granny Wendy was looking cross-eyed and confused, but George had spotted something he thought might help.

What has George found to help Granny?

WHAT'S WHAT &
WHO'S WHO OF
WITCHCRAFT

OLD SPELLS FOR SALE.
The Olde Curiosity Shop,
Witch Way, Wands Worth.

GREEN FROGS and tiny
toads always in stock at
The Pond, Green Witch Common.

SLIPPERY SLIME trick
performed by the one &
only Misty East. Tel: 9556

WITCH HAZEL
will magic away your
warts. Cauldron Castle,
Spell City.

LOOKING FOR THAT
SPECIAL SPELL? Visit
the Great Wise Wizard.
Look for this sign.

9

Star Flight

"Let's go!" cried George. "Let's visit the Great Wise Wizard! Maybe he'll give you a few witchy lessons too."

"I can't do that. He's famous. He's the cleverest wizard in the world." Granny Wendy looked shocked. But she really had nothing to lose. Maybe it was worth a try.

The Great Wise Wizard's castle was a long way away. "We'll have to fly there on my trusty broom," said Granny Wendy. "Jump up."

George and Lily were not too sure, especially when the broomstick wobbled wildly as they climbed aboard.

"Abracadabra, diddly-day," Granny chanted. "Take us to the Great Wise Wizz wa . . . Oops! I'm a little muddled."

Too late. The broomstick jolted up and down a few times then zoomed up into the sky. Distant stars rushed even closer.

"We're on the Great Wizzy Way," Granny exclaimed. "I don't know where to go from here. Maybe a signpost will help. Can you remember the sign we have to look for?"

Which signpost should they follow?

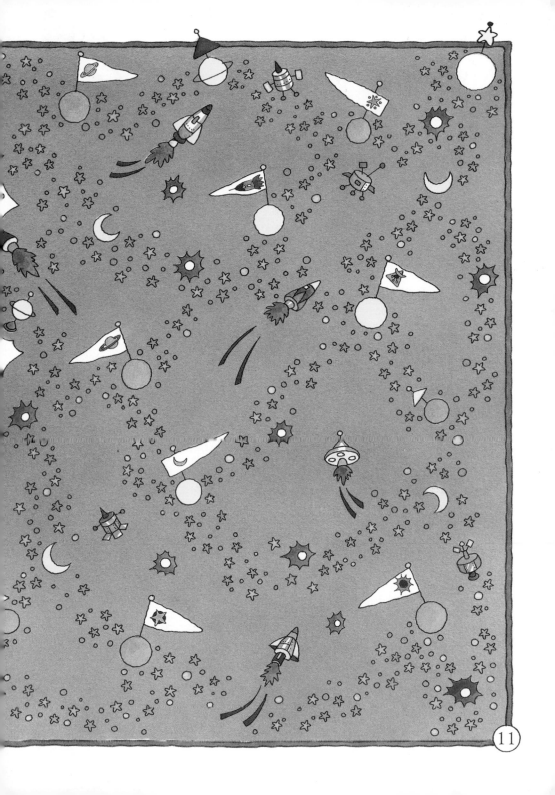

Mysterious Map

The broomstick zoomed off at lightning speed, skimming stars, before it shot back down to earth, crash-landing beside a huge old boot.

"Must belong to a giant," said Granny, picking herself up. "Oh no, we're in trouble. My broomstick is broken."

But they were in luck. Two big beads from the end of the giant laces were just what they needed to fix the broomstick. "It's a bit wobbly," said Granny. "But I think it'll work. Now, where are we?"

As if in answer, a large bird appeared and hovered just above their heads. It held a scroll of paper in its beak. George caught a glowing glass ball, like a giant marble, that fell from the scroll. Granny unrolled it to discover a picture map.

"A mountain with a big boot on top!" Granny
exclaimed. "That's where we are. And look, there's
the Wise Wizard's sign. He must live there."
"Perhaps he sent us the map," said Lily.
"Could he know we're on our way?"
George looked at the glowing
marble and had a funny feeling they
were being watched. And he was
right. The Great Wise Wizard was
keeping a close eye on them.

**Which is the mountain where the
Great Wise Wizard lives?**

Mountain Maze

George tucked the giant marble into his pocket and they set off. Lily kept watch for giants and held on tightly. The broomstick jolted even more than usual and didn't feel very safe.

It was a bumpy ride, but they were soon preparing to land at the bottom of the mountain where the Great Wise Wizard lived.

"We have to get to the entrance at the top of the mountain," said Granny Wendy. "But my broomstick is too wobbly. We'd better walk instead. It looks quite tricky and we'll have to steer clear of those red monsters. They don't look very friendly."

Can you find a way to the entrance at the top of the mountain?

Ice Cavern

They stepped through the entrance at the top of the
mountain and were amazed to find themselves inside a
glistening ice cavern which sparkled like diamonds.

"I can see a castle," exclaimed George. "That must be
where the Wizard lives."

George ran two paces and fell sprawling on the
slippery, glassy floor. Lily helped him to his feet and slowly
they made their way up to the castle.

Can you find your way along the paths to the castle?

The Key to the Castle

The castle towered above them.
"I wonder how we get in?"
Granny pondered.
There were four doors in the
weird rocks in front of them.
Perhaps one of these was the way
in? Lily tried but all were locked.
Again George had the
eerie feeling they were
being watched. In his
pocket the giant
marble was
getting hot.

He took it out and to his amazement the marble hovered in the air and sprouted three little antennae.

George looked at the marble, then he looked at the doors in the rocks. There were picture symbols on each one. Suddenly he had a brilliant idea. If he slotted the marble into one of the pictures it would make the sign of the Great Wise Wizard. Of course! The marble was a magic key.

Do you know which door it will open?

Inside the Castle

When the door creaked open they did not know what to expect, but certainly not the sunny garden that lay before them. They stepped down into a courtyard and only then saw a gardener holding a sad-looking pig in his arms.

Granny Wendy took one look at the poor little piglet and the half-eaten rhubarb leaf and guessed the problem. She rummaged in her pockets and whisked out a bottle of medicine.

"Three drops of this and he'll soon be fit," she said. The mixture worked like magic and the piglet happily trotted off to find his friends. The man looked impressed. Granny gave him the rest of the bottle. "Never more than three drops a day," she said.

"Cool," George whispered to Lily. Granny Wendy might have trouble with her spells, but she was a whiz with animals and plants. "Now where's the Wizard?"

"I think we've already found him," said Lily. "Though he's not quite what I expected."

"Don't be silly," said George. "Wizards don't look like that. He's the gardener, isn't he?"

What do you think?
Could he be the Great Wise Wizard?

The Book of Special Spells

There was a puff of smoke and the man stood transformed, looking much more like a Great Wise Wizard should.

"Visitors! How nice," he exclaimed. "No one's been here since two years last Tuesday."

The Wizard led the way inside his castle. "Please call me Douglas. All my friends do . . . it's my name, you know."

Soon they were standing inside a vast chamber. "Thank you for helping my pig," said Douglas. "Now perhaps I can help you. Let me fix this for a start."

Before their very eyes, the broomstick became whole again. "The secret of successful broomstickery is to get your magic words right," he smiled.

"That . . . and a little wizard dust." He sprinkled something sparkly onto the broom.

Then he magicked up a wizard snack for Lily and George and led Granny off to give her a few tips for her spell test.

The Wizard's tips were just what Granny Wendy needed. Her broomstick hovered in the air without so much as a shake or wobble.

"With a little practice, you'll be as good as any witch I know," Douglas said.

Then he unlocked a cupboard and took out a dusty old book. "My book of special spells," he said. "Why not try this one." He pointed to an open page. "But you'll have to decipher it yourself."

Granny Wendy looked puzzled for a moment. Then Lily saw Douglas sprinkle a little dust onto Granny's hat and at once, Granny smiled. "I've got it!" she exclaimed.

Can you decipher the spell?

gloop golden of
cup a and corn
of handfuls three
with Mix. acorn
magic a and
toadstool spotted
red a: flower

shaped bell-blue
a; teeth dragon's
two; cobweb one
Take: egg golden
a lay to goose
your get to
spell Special

23

The Enchanted Forest

"I've already got two of the ingredients," said Granny, pulling cobwebs and dragons' teeth from her pocket.

"All good witches carry those," said Douglas. "I have corn and golden gloop and you can take one of my geese. The only place to find the magic acorn, flower and toadstool is the Enchanted Forest. But you'll have to hurry."

They said goodbye and set off smoothly on the broomstick.

They found the Enchanted Forest. It was a strange place. Wild animal calls rang out and curious plants grew everywhere. George and Lily would have liked to explore but they had no time. The toadstool was easy to spot, but the flower and acorn were more tricky.

Can you find them?

Lift Off!

At last, Granny Wendy had everything she needed but it was now nearly time for the spell test.

"Come on Granny," cried Lily as they leaped onto the broomstick. "We can do it."

The broomstick seemed to have a mind of its own, zooming along at breakneck speed, looping the loop and skimming the clouds.

Lily remembered the powder Douglas had sprinkled over it and wondered if that had anything to do with it. "We're supersonic," she gasped as they overtook a jet.

The broomstick dived earthwards, skidding to a stop as the clock struck twelve. Granny straightened her hat. She tucked the goose under her arm and gulped. This was it. Time for her test. But there was a surprise in store for her when she saw the panel of testers.

Do you recognize anyone?

Granny's Test

The test began. Nervously, Granny Wendy mixed the ingredients for her special spell and set them to simmer while she carried on with the other tasks. First she pulled a fluffy rabbit out of her cauldron, then her broomstick hovered perfectly.

Next, she uttered the magic words to make George invisible. This was quite tricky and at first nothing happened. Granny said the words again. Still nothing. She tried again.

This time Granny concentrated so hard that her hat suddenly took off. It whizzed into orbit around the room which was lucky as George had almost but not quite disappeared.

Lily jumped in to hide what was left of him while everyone else watched the whizzing hat ~ all except Douglas who giggled.

Granny was worn out by her efforts. Now all that was left was to try out her special mix on the goose. Would it work? There was silence. Everyone waited. Time ticked on until the goose hiccuped and there it was. The goose was sitting on a golden egg.

Everyone gazed at the golden egg, so no one noticed two shoes tiptoe behind the table. George was still almost invisible and he wanted to check Granny's marks. She needed 25 to pass.

Has Granny made it? How many marks has she got?

5 6 4 7 5

Granny Gets it Right

Granny Wendy could hardly believe it. She had passed her test. Now she could keep her hat and broomstick. Best of all she was a real witch at last.

Granny jumped for joy. "Come on," she called to George and Lily. "I'll take you for a celebratory spin on my broomstick."

They were about to set off when a familiar figure came bounding down the school steps, waving wildly. "Wait for me!" yelled Douglas. "I don't want to miss all the fun. I'm coming too."

Answers

Pages 4-5

Granny has dropped her spell book. It is circled below.

Pages 6-7

The Spell Library card is circled below.

Pages 8-9

George has spotted something in the open book. It says that if you need a special spell you should visit the Great Wise Wizard.

Pages 10-11

The signpost they should follow is

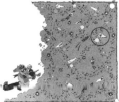

circled below. It's the only one with Wizard's sign on it.

Pages 12-13

The mountain where the Great Wise Wizard lives is circled below.

Pages 14-15

The way to the entrance at the top of the mountain is marked here.

Pages 16-17

The way along the paths to the castle is marked here.

Pages 18-19

The key will open the door circled below. The glass ball fits the carving on it to make the Great Wise Wizard's sign.

Pages 20-21

The man is indeed the Great Wise Wizard. We know this because he has the Wizard's symbol on his pocket. It is circled here.

Pages 22-23

The spell is written the wrong way around. Start at the bottom of the right-hand page and read up. Then go onto the bottom of the left-hand page and read up. It says:
To get your goose to lay a golden egg: Take one cobweb, two dragon's teeth, a blue bell-shaped flower, a red spotted toadstool and a magic acorn. Mix with three handfuls of corn and a cup of golden gloop.

Pages 24-25

The toadstool, the flower and the acorn are circled below.

Pages 26-27

The Great Wise Wizard is one of the judges. He is the one in the middle. The Head Wizard and Head Witch are there too.

Pages 28-29

Granny has 27 marks, so she has passed the test.

This edition first published in 2002 by Usborne Publishing Ltd., Usborne House, 83-85 Saffron Hill, London EC1N 8RT, England. www.usborne.com Copyright © 2002, 1995 Usborne Publishing Ltd. The name Usborne and the devices ♈ 🌐 are Trade Marks of Usborne Publishing Ltd. All rights reserved.